Even Higher!

A Rosh Hashanah Story by I. L. Peretz

Adapted by Eric A. Kimmel ✶ *Illustrated by* Jill Weber

Holiday House / New York

In memory of our dear friend Coleen Salley.
Life is well worth living.   —E. A. K.

To Papa, my grandfather who came here from
Russia when he was 13   —J. W.

Title page hand lettering by Anthony Bloch

Text copyright © 2009 by Eric A. Kimmel
Illustrations copyright © 2009 by Jill Weber
All Rights Reserved
HOLIDAY HOUSE is registered in the U.S. Patent and Trademark Office.
Printed in the United States of America
The text typeface is Hightower Roman.
The artwork was created with gouache, gesso, watercolor, ink, colored pencils,
and caran d'ache wax crayons.
www.holidayhouse.com
First Edition
1 3 5 7 9 10 8 6 4 2

Library of Congress Cataloging-in-Publication Data
Kimmel, Eric A.
Even higher! / a Rosh Hashanah story by I.L. Peretz ;
adapted by Eric A. Kimmel ; illustrated by Jill Weber. — 1st ed.
p. cm.
Summary: A skeptical visitor to the village of Nemirov finds out where its
rabbi really goes just before the Jewish New Year, when the villagers claim
he goes to heaven to speak to God.
ISBN 978-0-8234-2020-9 (hardcover)
[1. Jews—Folklore. 2. Folklore.] I. Weber, Jill, ill. II. Peretz, Isaac Leib, 1851
or 2-1915. Oyb nisht nokh hekher. III. Title.
PZ8.1.K567Ev 2009
398.2—dc21
[E]
2008019710

Where did the rabbi go? Every year, during the days before Rosh Hashanah, the rabbi of Nemirov disappeared. He wasn't in his house. He wasn't in the synagogue. He wasn't in the market.

Where was he?

The people of Nemirov thought they knew. They were certain that the rabbi went to heaven. Where else would he go? Everyone knew that on Rosh Hashanah God opens the Book of Life and decides the fate of every living soul for the coming year.

On Rosh Hashanah it is written and on Yom Kippur it is sealed. Who will be raised up, and who will be brought low. Who will rest in one place, and who will wander.

Prayer, charity, and repentance could save a soul from misfortune. But there were so many souls in need of forgiveness and so little time for their prayers to be heard and their good deeds to be recorded.

So, of course the rabbi went
to heaven: to beg and plead with
God to forgive each soul. And
God listened, because the rabbi
of Nemirov was a great and
holy man.

Now it happened that a Litvak came to town. A Litvak is what we call a person from Lithuania. But the word means more than that. It means a scoffer, a doubter—one who does not believe in miracles. This Litvak was a true Litvak—a complete skeptic.

You mustn't think he was not religious. No, he was a pious man and a learned one.

But whenever someone in town talked about a miracle he had seen with his own eyes, this Litvak would quote from the writings of ten famous rabbis, proving that it could not happen.

So, naturally, when the people of Nemirov talked about their rabbi going to heaven, the Litvak refused to believe it. "The Bible teaches that only Enoch and Elijah went to heaven in their lifetimes. Are you saying that your rabbi is as great as Elijah?"

"Scoffer! All we know is that our rabbi goes to heaven before Rosh Hashanah. If he doesn't, where else does he go?"

"He doesn't go to heaven," the Litvak insisted.

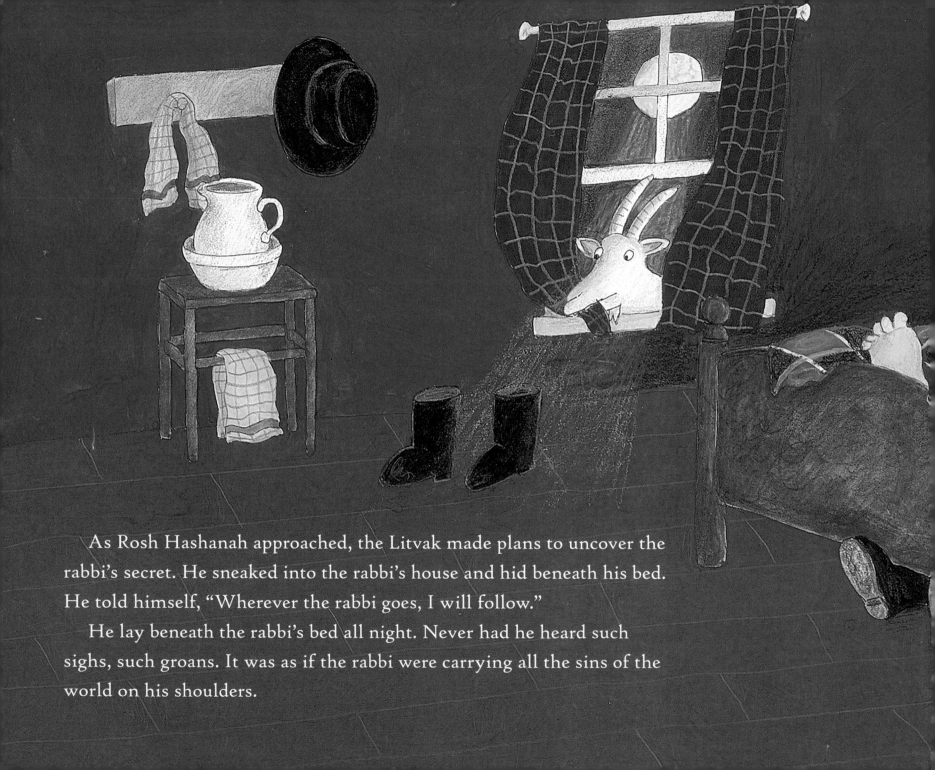

As Rosh Hashanah approached, the Litvak made plans to uncover the rabbi's secret. He sneaked into the rabbi's house and hid beneath his bed. He told himself, "Wherever the rabbi goes, I will follow."

He lay beneath the rabbi's bed all night. Never had he heard such sighs, such groans. It was as if the rabbi were carrying all the sins of the world on his shoulders.

The Litvak trembled, but he stayed where he was.

Two hours before dawn, the rabbi got up. He washed, said his morning prayers, then went to his closet. The Litvak watched as the rabbi put on the rough, homespun clothes of a peasant:

a linen blouse and trousers, tall boots,
a wide leather belt, a long woolen coat,
and a greasy sheepskin cap.

The rabbi tied a rope
around his waist and
walked out the door.

The Litvak followed, stepping quietly on tiptoes. He watched the rabbi pick up a hatchet lying beside the woodpile and followed him through the silent streets of the sleeping town, all the way to the forest. "Wherever he's going, it isn't heaven," the Litvak sneered.

The rabbi walked to a part of the forest where several trees had blown over in a windstorm. The wood was dry, well seasoned. As the Litvak watched, the rabbi chopped off the larger branches, splitting them into firewood and kindling. He tied the wood together and hoisted the heavy bundle onto his back.

"Is he going to sell wood in the marketplace?" the Litvak wondered as he followed the rabbi back to town.

The rabbi turned down a crooked alley filled with trash and sewage. Rags stuffed the holes in the broken windowpanes. The crumbling houses leaned together in misery. The Litvak hesitated. Why was the rabbi here?

The rabbi stopped before a wretched shack.
He knocked on the door. A weak voice inside
groaned, "Who's there?"

"Hey, old girl! Who do you think it is? It's
your pal Vasilly the woodcutter. I got some
prime wood for you. It'll burn like the devil in
your stove."

The Litvak was shocked. How could a rabbi,
a holy man, talk in such a crude manner?

"Go away," said the person inside. "How can I buy any wood? I'm old. I'm sick. I don't have any money."

The rabbi pushed open the door. The Litvak looked through the window. He saw an ancient woman, thin as a stick of kindling, lying on the floor.

"Of course you're sick, Grandma!" the rabbi said, dropping his bundle. "This house is freezing. Get a good fire going and you'll feel better. Look! I got stove wood and kindling. Only six kopecks for the bundle. Don't tell me you don't have that!"

"I don't."

"So? You'll pay me later. Don't you think that mighty, powerful God you pray to can't somehow come up with six crummy pennies to help a poor old woman buy firewood?"

Brrr
Brrr

"All right. Leave the wood. But how am I going to light it? I'm too sick to get out of bed."

"Silly girl! I'll light you such a fire, you'll jump up and dance!"

As the Litvak watched, the rabbi arranged the wood and the kindling in the stove. He struck a match and sang in a low, sad tone:

"*Let's go, buddies. Up the road There's a tavern waiting....*"

As the flames rose and the kindling caught fire, he sang in a louder voice:

"Light a fire on the stove. All our pals are singing...."

The wood began to crackle. Heat filled the room.
Sparks rose from the stove to float in the air like
dancing balls of light. And Vasilly the woodcutter,
who was really the rabbi of Nemirov, pulled the
old woman from her pallet on the floor and
whirled her around in a circle. Together
they began to sing and dance.

The Litvak did not wait to see more. He ran through the streets until he reached his room. There he remained for three days.

The Litvak became a follower of
the rabbi of Nemirov that Rosh
Hashanah. He remained one for
the rest of his life. Never again
did he scoff at miracles. And
whenever he heard someone
say that on the days before
Rosh Hashanah the rabbi
of Nemirov flew up to
heaven, he would nod
his head and add in a
quiet voice,

"Who knows?
Maybe even higher!"

AUTHOR'S NOTE

Isaac Leib Peretz (1852–1915) stands as one of the giants of modern Jewish literature. "If Not Higher" ("Oyb Nit Nokh Hekher") is one of his most famous stories. The miracle is that there are no miracles. We don't need them. Ordinary kindness and compassion are enough to save the world.

In adapting this story, I incorporated a Ukrainian drinking song that has become a hymn for the Rosh Hashanah holiday: "Let's go, buddies. Up the road / There's a tavern waiting. . . ." The tavern is Paradise. There we'll drink the Water of Life.

In the original story, the old woman doesn't get out of bed. I let her dance in memory of the time when my grandmother, at eighty-five, pulled me out of a kitchen chair and tried to teach me to dance the Krakowska Wesele.